Iris is the resident artist of the garden. Although she is very shy and quiet, her deep emotions show on her wonderful canvases.

Pitterpat is a fluffy and devoted kitten. She and Rose-Petal have an extra-special relationship and are rarely seen apart. Pitterpat has saved Rose-Petal from trouble on more than one occasion.

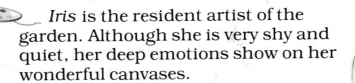

P.D. Centipede, the athlete of Rose-Petal Place, sees life as one big game. He is full of pep, and can be seen jogging around the garden every morning.

Seymour J. Snailsworth is a snail of great wisdom. He carries his unique and elegant home on his back, and can always be called upon for a word or two of advice.

Tumbles the Hedgehog is a happy-go-lucky fellow who is always full of fun and laughs. The girls love to have Tumbles around, even if he does trip and stumble a lot!

Unfortunately, there is a dark and untended part of the garden where nothing grows. There, in Tin-Can Castle, live *Nastina,* an evil spider, and her hateful assistant, *Horace Fly.* Nastina's goal in life is to get rid of Rose-Petal and make herself Queen of Rose-Petal Place. So we are always on our guard against Nastina and her wicked tricks.

With all of us working and playing together, Rose-Petal Place remains an enchanted garden full of sunshine and flowers, music and laughter. Please come join us!

Library of Congress Cataloging in Publication Data: Johnson, Hedvig. Love Helps You Grow. Rose-Petal Place. SUMMARY: Orchid's jealousy of Sunny Sunflower is exacerbated by Nastina, and only the combined love of all the garden inhabitants is able to put things right.
[1. Gardens—Fiction.   2. Jealousy—Fiction]   I. Title.   II. Series.
PZ7.J63196Ev   1984   [E]   83-27315   ISBN 0-910313-58-X
Manufactured in the United States of America 1 2 3 4 5 6 7 8 9 0

ROSE-PETAL PLACE™

Love Helps
You Grow

by Hedvig Johnson
Pictures by Pat Paris and Jeanie Shackelford

"Wake up, lovely plants,
Wash your faces with dew,
Smile up at the sun,
The day's dawning on you."

The sun was just peering over the east of the garden when Rose-Petal's beautiful good-morning song rang out.

Sunny Sunflower and Orchid ran hand in hand up the flagstone path to find her.

"Good morning, Orchid," smiled Rose-Petal, "and good morning, Sunny. I have never seen you look lovelier, Sunny!"

"Do you really like my new dress, Rose-Petal?"

"The color and style are perfect for you! You are as bright as sunlight itself, Sunny."

Rose-Petal and Sunny Sunflower were so busy chatting that neither of them noticed Orchid slip away. She ran toward the far end of the garden, sobbing and sniffing, and brushing the tears from her eyes with her little clenched fists.

"Rose-Petal always compliments Sunny, but she never says anything nice to me!" she cried.

Horace Fly, out for his early morning scouting trip, noticed her distress and asked, "What's your problem, Orchid?"

"It's none of your business, Horace!"

"You can trust me. I'm your friend. Maybe I can help." Horace sounded sincere.

Orchid's problem spilled out in a rush of words between sobs.

"That Sunny Sunflower! She thinks she's so pretty! And Rose-Petal loves her more than anyone else . . . and pays more attention to her . . . and smiles at her . . . and . . ."

"That's awful! How unfair! All of you girls
should be treated alike. I'll bet Nastina could
help you get even with Sunny and Rose-Petal for
being so thoughtless."

"Why on earth would Nastina help me?"
sniffed Orchid.

"Well, I'll talk to her and let you know."
Wanting to be alone in her misery, Orchid hid behind a large mulberry bush. Horace scurried off to dreary Tin-Can Castle, Nastina's home.

"Nastina, I know something you'd like to know."

"Well don't buzz around me, stupid, speak up!" snapped Nastina.

"I just saw Orchid crying her eyes out. Her feelings are hurt because Rose-Petal said something nice to Sunny Sunflower. Right now Orchid's hiding out trying to figure out how to get even with Sunny."

"Aha! Jealousy has struck one of those perfect creatures! Heh, heh, heh! I know how to handle that. I'll cast a spell on Orchid, and Rose-Petal will have to come to me for help. Maybe, at last, we'll get rid of those pests. Horace, for once in your life, you've brought me some good news! Let's find Orchid."

But when Nastina and Horace found Orchid crying behind the mulberry bush, she was so upset about what Rose-Petal had said to Sunny Sunflower that she could hardly talk. All she could think about were her feelings about her two friends and how they had treated her.

"There, there, you poor child, I'll help you," said Nastina soothingly, as she gently patted Orchid's shoulder. "I can solve your problem, but you must trust me. Will you let me hold both of your hands?"

Orchid was so unhappy and confused that she was glad to hear some kind words, even if they did come from Nastina. She hesitated for a moment, but then put her hands into two of Nastina's.

"Now, have a little drink to calm your nerves, dearie," cooed Nastina, handing Orchid a silver goblet full of an evil potion she had prepared.

"Well, I am thirsty," said Orchid, and she drank it down.

After Orchid had finished drinking, Nastina looked at her and began to chant:

"Jealousy, jealousy,
Do your trick,
Belittle this lassie,
Quick, quick, quick!"

Orchid suddenly became very quiet. She didn't understand what was happening, but she hoped that Nastina would be able to help her.

Nastina went on, "The first thing I want you to do is find your friends and tell them how thoughtless Rose-Petal and Sunny Sunflower are. Go, now, bring them here, but don't tell them that you've seen Horace and me."

Obediently, Orchid went to find Lily Fair, Iris, and Daffodil. On her way, she saw Pitterpat, Tumbles the Hedgehog, and P. D. Centipede playing hide-and-seek among the tiger lilies.

"I have something important to talk about.
Will you three find Seymour J. Snailsworth?
Then all of you meet me by the mulberry bush in
a little while," she said nervously.

P. D. said, "We'll all be there, Orchid."

Orchid hurried on.

"I wonder why she was so upset?" P. D. Centipede said out loud. "I guess we'll find out soon enough. But I smell trouble!"

Soon Iris, Lily Fair, and Daffodil came
hurrying down the path to join the others at the
mulberry bush. They all formed a circle around
Orchid and waited for her to speak. None of
them saw Nastina and Horace lurking behind
the bushes.

Orchid began her story. "I want to tell you all about Sunny Sunflower and Rose-Petal. That Sunny — she is so-o-o vain! She thinks she's prettier than all of us!"

The listeners were surprised to hear Orchid saying such jealous, unhappy things about Sunny. Something strange seemed to be happening to Orchid, too. She actually was shrinking right before their eyes!

Without even taking a deep breath, Orchid
went on. "Rose-Petal is always giving Sunny
compliments."

The group watched in horror as Orchid began to shrink faster and faster. She had become no larger than a pea. Her voice was getting more and more shrill.

"What's happening to you, Orchid?" screamed Lily Fair.

"There's nothing wrong with me," piped Orchid, in a teeny-tiny shrill voice. "Can't you see, it's Rose-Petal and Sunny that are spoiling everything with . . ."

Orchid's voice trailed away, as she shrank down to the size of an ant.

For a moment all her friends stood still as statues. They stared in disbelief at the spot where tiny little Orchid was standing.

Then from behind the mulberry bush came
the mocking voice of Nastina.

"Heh, heh, heh! I wonder what Rose-Petal will
think of this! Tell her I can make Orchid grow —
for a price, that is! Heh, heh, heh!"

The mocking voice of Nastina spurred the little
group to action. They rushed through the
garden crying for Rose-Petal. Even Seymour
moved at his fastest snail pace.

"My goodness! What's the trouble?" asked Rose-Petal.

"Something terrible has happened to Orchid!" Daffodil cried.

"And we know who's to blame!" added Lily Fair.

"I couldn't believe what Orchid said," Iris stated.

"Would one of you please tell me what's going on?" exclaimed Rose-Petal. "I can't make sense out of any of this!"

By this time Seymour had joined the group. Rose-Petal turned to him.

"Seymour, will you tell me, please?"

In his logical way, Seymour told Rose-Petal about how upset and jealous Orchid had been and about the evil spell Nastina had cast on Orchid that had reduced her to the size of an ant!

When he told of Nastina's part in the affair, Rose-Petal said, "I bet I know her price for restoring Orchid to full size. She means to drive us all from the garden!"

They looked at one another unhappily.

"What can we do?" asked Sunny Sunflower. "I feel it's all my fault. I'll do anything to help!"

"Getting Orchid back is our greatest task. We must rescue her without Nastina's help. We know Nastina wants to get rid of all of us," said Rose-Petal seriously.

"Jealousy is such a bad feeling," commented Sunny Sunflower. "It can make a big, nice person small."

"It certainly is a bad feeling," said Rose-Petal, especially since everyone is beautiful in their own way. But I know something even stronger than jealousy. Love!! Love is stronger than anything. It's stronger than Nastina or her wicked spells. How many of you truly love Orchid?"

Every hand was raised.

"Please take me to her. I'd like all of you to come along."

A silent, thoughtful group returned to the mulberry bush.

"Let's make a ring of love around Orchid. We'll all hold hands while I sing to her."

"Beautiful Orchid,
Return to us, do.
We truly love you,
Please love us all, too.
Beautiful Orchid,
Push jealousy away.
We'll all feel much better,
If love rules each day."

"I love you, Rose-Petal," Orchid peeped in her
teeny-tiny voice. "I love you, too, Sunny. You do
look beautiful today."

Her voice became stronger with each word. Their wondering eyes saw her slowly grow to her own size again.

She hugged everyone, smiling through happy tears.

"I was so silly to be jealous. Can you ever forgive me?"

Rose-Petal spoke for all of them when she said quietly, "We love you, Orchid. There's nothing to forgive. And now let's all agree to stop jealousy from spoiling our beautiful garden ever again."

"Hurray!" shouted all the girls.

Nastina and Horace watched the happy, chattering group skip up the garden walk. Nastina turned to Horace, "Can you believe that bunch? They're all so sweet they make me sick!"

Then she boxed him soundly on each side of his head. "That's for telling me about that stupid girl and her troubles," she said.

"Let's all sing together again to celebrate this happy occasion!" called Orchid, happily.

Everyone agreed, and the sound of their lovely voices reached to the farthest corner of Rose-Petal Place:

"Beautiful Orchid
You've pushed jealousy away.
We all feel much better,
Because love rules each day."

Welcome to Rose-Petal Place!

I'm Elmer the elm tree, and I know everything there is to know about this beautiful garden because I keep it all recorded in my diary. Let me introduce you to the delightful group of characters who have made Rose-Petal Place their home.

Rose-Petal is the natural leader and protector of Rose-Petal Place. She is as talented as she is beautiful and sweet. Her magical singing keeps the garden blooming, and her good common sense keeps everyone in it safe and happy.

Sunny Sunflower is Rose-Petal's best friend. As is often the case with best friends, they are opposites in many ways. Sunny is a tomboy who always says exactly what's on her mind. You might say she's "spice" to Rose-Petal's "sugar."

Lily Fair is a dreamer whose dearest wish is to be a star. She is sincere and dedicated and can be seen practicing her dancing at all hours of the day and night.

Daffodil is all business. She runs the Bouquet Boutique, where all the girls go for their beautiful clothes. She has big plans for her future as a businesswoman and is never without her flower-shaped calculator.

Orchid is Daffodil's best customer. She loves to pamper herself and spends most of her time on self-improvement. When Orchid is not actually shopping, she is thinking about it!